Little Fox
and the Island
of Parrots

Rowan Sylva & Daniela Gast

Bean Sprout
Press

We would like to express our gratitude to the Ministry for Science, Research and Culture, Land Brandenburg, Germany, for providing funding for this project.

Beansprout Press,
an imprint of Lasavia Publishing Ltd.
Auckland, New Zealand

www.lasaviapublishing.com

ISBN: 978-1-99-116051-5

Chapter 1 - Pobo the Platypus

Little Fox and Yellow Belly the snake were enjoying a meal of grilled fish beside the little stream while the meadow buzzed with the life of early spring.

"This is the life," said Yellow Belly as he stretched out in the weak sun. "Lying around all day, being lethargic, not doing a thing at all for months at a time. It's wonderful."

Little Fox sighed. "It's good and all, but don't you think it gets a bit boring?"

"Boring?" Yellow Belly rolled his eyes. "You warm blooded animals, you can't appreciate anything! You always have to run around and do stuff all day, like catching butterflies and longing for adventure. Can't you recognize the good life when you see it? Adventure is just another word for life threatening danger and horrifying stress. Learn to be more like me. I just alternate between hibernation and sunbathing."

"I suppose you are right," said Little Fox as he looked wistfully down the river, wondering where it went. "Hey," said Little Fox suddenly, "What's that?"

Yellow Belly peered down the river. "I don't know but its getting closer."

The two animals sat and watched the brown smudge traveling upriver. The wind blew from the south, and little Fox got a whiff of a smell he knew not: salty, musky, and adventurous. "I think," said little Fox, "it's a little boat. There's an animal on it and its being pulled by a pair of salmon."

"It looks like a cross between a rat and a duck," said Yellow Belly.

The fox and the snake watched in amazement as a little canoe drew near. A bizarre looking animal, about a third the size of Little Fox, tied his boat to a birch sapling, unhitched the salmon and waved them good bye. He then waddled over to the two animals. He had an eye patch over one eye and wore a belt from which dangled a variety of things: a compass, a spyglass, a sword, and a length of rope.

"Greetings, I am Pobo the Platypus," said the creature. "Am I right in addressing Little Fox, hero of the Rain Sticks and saviour of the Moonstone Mountains?"

Little Fox blushed beneath his red and white fur.

"Hey rat-duck," said Yellow Belly, "you forgot about the amazing snake."

Pobo glared at Yellow Belly, obviously not happy about being called a rat-duck. "Don't get your tail in a twist. I have also heard that you are

5

small and harmless for a snake. I've seen snakes that can swallow a deer and others so venomous that they can paralyse a lion. As it is," said Pogo menacingly, "I'm probably more venomous than you." The platypus indicated a nasty looking spur protruding from his ankles. Anyway I'm here to ask for help. I've accepted a mission to find a hero, and I need the best. And word on the high seas is that's you."

Chapter 2 –
the plight of Parrot Island

"Let me get this straight," said Yellow Belly. "You have a ship and you sail around. Why?"

"I trade stuff, you want fruits from a ningo tree? Who do you ask: old Pogo. You want elephant dung up north? Who do you ask: old Pogo. You want feathers from Parrot Island? Pogo's your animal. I've been all around the world. Not many animals can say they've been as far as Pogo."

"And are there many more of you platypie out there?"

Pogo scowled, "Not platipie, not platipod, and not platipussies. Platypuses are what we are called."

"Yes okay," said Little Fox, "but what about Parrot Island? I want to know more."

"Ahh," said Pogo a smile stretching across his bill. "It's a paradise: always warm, so many fruits, beautiful water to swim in, no predators to speak of. The parrots are a matriarchal society. That means the girls and ladies are the bosses and they always make sure that life is fun and peaceful. I owe the high parrot priestess my life and my heart."

"Always warm you say?" said Yellow Belly. "That does sound good."

"But what do they need a hero for?" said Little Fox.

"Well that's the tragedy. Parrot Island is slowly sinking into the sea. Already the mangrove trees are becoming submerged. The trouble all started when smoke began to pour from the top of the volcano that is in the middle of the island. The gods, they say, are angry. That was why I agreed to find a hero to help and why I've come to you. If you'll agree, I'll take you to my ship and then I'll take you to the island itself to see what you can do. Of course if its treasure and riches you're after, the high priestess will reward you."

"Of course we'll help you," said Little Fox excitedly. "No need to offer a reward. We'll do all we can to help the good parrots."

Yellow Belly rose up on his coils and gave Little Fox a hard look. "Can we talk in private?"

Pobo shrugged and wandered a short distance off.

"Are you crazy?" said Yellow Belly. "We don't even know who this rat-duck guy is, or even if we can trust him. Even if he is telling the truth, we'll be going further from home than we have ever gone before. There is a good chance we will never come back. And we'll be at sea. I can't speak for Duck-Rat, but we're land animals. It's not natural."

"Oh come on," said Little Fox. "You're just sour because he called you small and harmless. Think about the amazing things we'll see. Think of all the sun you will be able to soak up. Also I don't think he likes being called Rat-Duck."

"I'm not going," said Yellow Belly.

Chapter 3 - The Green River

Despite Yellow Belly's complaints, he did in the end agree to go. And despite the fact that Yellow Belly and Pobo were snarky with each other, the three animals had a pleasant journey downstream. Yellow Belly swam, the platypus floated in his canoe and Little Fox ran alongside. Through the meadow and scrubland they journeyed until they came to the swamps of Stinkdom. Here the frogs led them through the sluggish streams. They were given a warm welcome by Slimey, who dutifully supplied them with a couple of recently deceased relatives. Which Yellow Belly found delicious and Little Fox had to admit weren't bad roasted on a fire. Pobo preferred to share the flies with the frogs,

muttering something about carnivores.

The next morning the animals continued their journey. The river that flowed out of the swamps was bigger than the stream. Soon it became deep, wide and green. There, tied to some alders, was a strange floating construction. It was a raft with a couple of ramshackle houses, a tower and a big white flag, hanging limp in the still air.

"Well here we are," said Pobo, as he dived off his canoe and poked his head out of the water, "my ship,

the Monotreme. It'll take us down the Green River to the sea in no time."

"That's your ship?" said Yellow Belly, as he shot through the water. "That beaver dam is seaworthy?"

"What would you know about seaworthy?" said Pobo. "Think you're a sea serpent now do ya?"

Yellow Belly looked beneath him and saw a large dark shadow looming up from the depths. He screamed and flew straight out of the water and into the air. He cartwheeled before falling with a splash back in to the river.

Pobo laughed, accidently breathed in water and spluttered.

Little Fox watched from tree roots at the edge of the river as a beautiful silvery dolphin surfaced and leapt into the sky before diving back under.

"That's Sheila," shouted Pobo, "Don't you worry your pretty little head about her, snake. She and her sister, Moonbeam, are going to pull this ship all the way to Parrot Island.

Once they were all onboard and comfortable the two dolphins

fitted themselves into harnesses and pulled the boat out into the river. The animals watched the landscape drift by. They journeyed past rolling hills and various riverside animal dwellings. They had to stop at the sprawling Beaver Town to pay tolls. Pobo paid with a chunk of ambergris, a stone from a whale's belly.

"The beavers love it," Pobo said. "The boys use it as perfume to smell good for the girls."

After Beaver Town the banks of the river grew

swampy again with lots of reeds
and grasses.

"The herons and shags rule
here," said Pobo. "They're alright.
They let a traveler mind their business."

Night fell and Yellow Belly and Little Fox fell
asleep on mats while Pobo stayed awake talking to
the dolphins.

Chapter 4 - The Great Ocean

Before long their journey led them to the sand dunes
that ran along the swampy delta that led to the sea
and out to Jellyfish Bay. Jellyfish Bay had stony
beaches and was surrounded by high white cliffs
from which hung windswept pines and oaks. On
entering the salt-water, the dolphins abandoned the
ship for some hours to swim, play and hunt for fish.
Little Fox and Yellow Belly sat with Pobo on the
deck of his ship.

"So you can talk to the dolphins?" asked Little Fox.

"Oh yeah," said Pobo, "dolphins love talking. They're talking all the time."

"How come we can't hear them then?" asked Yellow Belly.

"Because they talk under the water, using special ultrasounds. I can receive the vibrations with electroreceptors on my bill and talk back to them."

"What do they talk about," asked Little Fox.

"Just about everything," said Pobo. "What they are going to eat, what they have just eaten, how can the corrupting effect of power be tempered by the democratic impulse, how much they are looking forward to the sea again, and," Pobo eyed Yellow Belly, "How suspicious they are of freshies."

"Freshies?" asked the snake.

"Fresh water animals like you. They're particularly interested in you, Snaky, what manner of water creature you are. You know, I think you might be able to talk to dolphins. You just go in the water and really open your ears. There's no hope for a fox though. You don't get more terrestrial than

17

that."

"hsss," said Yellow Belly. "Talking to dolphins huh. I kind of like the idea of that."

The first view days of their voyage passed uneventfully. Yellow Belly was seasick. And, without land in sight, Little Fox was also starting to feel a little nervous and afraid. After the third day the weather started to get rough. Black clouds rolled over the horizon, thunder rumbled, lightening shot across the sky, and what had been a slightly choppy ocean turned into hills and valleys of water.

"We're going to die," wailed Yellow Belly, as a wave crashed over the barge."

"Make yourselves useful," shouted Pobo as he clambered over his ship, in and out of the water, deconstructing the towers and lashing everything down with rope. "Find a sheltered spot and tie yourselves to the ship."

Little Fox found himself more frightened than when he had been carried in the talons of an eagle, as he clung to a pile of rope and wood, while freezing cold water sloshed over him. Eventually the storm ended. The ocean became flat and the sun warmed the cold, drenched animals lying on the deck of the ship.

Chapter 5 - Rough Town

"We're lost," moaned Yellow Belly as the sky met the ocean in every direction, and a hot breeze blew across the deck of the ship. "We'll soon die of thirst."

"Don't get your fangs in your flipper," said Pobo, "Sheila never gets lost. We're right on course and not too far from Red Ant Island, where we can put in at Rough Town for some supplies and repairs, before making the last haul to Parrot Island."

"Rough Town," muttered Yellow Belly, "I don't like the sound of that."

The animals sailed on until a green smudge appeared on the horizon. Little Fox was very happy to see land and he ran around the deck squealing. As they drew nearer, they could make out the island.

"Sugar plants," replied Pobo, when Little Fox asked about the strange looking grasses that grew all over the hills. "You got to get your sugar from somewhere. When you guys get to Rough Town go easy on the sugar juice."

Before long they pulled up at Rough Town. It was a collection of ramshackle huts and jetties going out into the water where an array of equally ramshackle ships were docked.

"You animals explore town," said Pobo after he had tied up his ship to a jetty and lowered the gangplank. "I'll organize the repairs. We'll sleep on

21

board tonight and continue our voyage tomorrow."

Yellow Belly rode on Little Foxes back while he raced up the gangplank, across the jetty and into the yellow dusty streets of the town. Along the water front were shops, from which animals sold various things: a warm water penguin selling sunken treasures, a one eyed sea rat selling crates of bird poo and a small fresh water crocodile selling smoked fish.

"I have to say," said Yellow Belly, "I think Rough Town is a great place. The heat." The snake flicked his tongue in and out of his mouth. "The tastes. Can we move here?"

"I don't like it," said Little Fox as he eyed two seagulls whispering to each other under the eaves of a hut. "The smells are all overwhelming. And

the animals are all drinking something. I suppose its sugar juice."

The two friends passed an open hut made from

bamboo where a loris was feeding stems of sugar into a grinder, out of which a dirty-green juice flowed into wooden bowls while a range of animals, including two green, girl tree-snakes drank.

"Hey," they called out to Yellow Belly, "Snake friend, come and have a drink with us in the sugar bar."

Yellow Belly took one look at Little Fox before diving toward the bar.

"Wait," said Little Fox, "remember what Pobo said!"

A few moments later Little Fox and Yellow Belly were settled in the bar. Little Fox was looking tensely around. Yellow Belly was chatting with the green trees snakes who were twisting tails around him while he slurped back a cup of sugar juice. Little Fox looked nervously around at the animals at

the bar. A squint-eyed marmoset grinned at Little Fox and jumped over to him, a bowl of sugar juice in his hand.

"You're traveling with old Pobo the Platypus, aren't ya?" the Marmoset grinned. His teeth were brown and rotting. "Mark my words, that platypus is a sweet talker but he's not to be trusted he's a two timing dung smuggler. Sugar?"

Little Fox slowly backed away.

"Try it try it," said the marmoset.

Little Fox took a sip from the bowl and a sweet flavor washed over him taking away the rough feeling of the voyage.

"There ya go," grinned the marmoset.

Chapter 6 - The Journey Continues

Little Fox and Yellow Belly woke up by the edge of the water.

"My head hurts," moaned Yellow Belly.

"Mine too," said Little Fox. "I told you we shouldn't have drunk all that sugar juice. Come on we need to get back to the ship. Pobo said he wanted to leave early and the sun is already well up."

"But wasn't that sugar good," said Yellow Belly as he curled himself around Little Fox's tail, "and the green tree snakes were so nice."

"I hardly remember any of it," said Little Fox as he ran along the waterfront.

"You were having a party," said Yellow Belly, "good to see for once. You were lapping the sugar juice off the table and telling all of those dodgy creatures about our mission and what a hero you were."

"I did not," said Little Fox.

"Yes you did," said Yellow Belly.

"Oh no…" said Little Fox. "I'm never drinking sugar juice again."

They got back to Pobo's ship where the platypus was pacing the deck and the dolphins were jumping in and out of the water.

"There you are," said Pobo, as Little Fox and Yellow Belly trotted up the gangplank.

"I feel like I'm going to be sick," said Little Fox.

Pobo's eyes narrowed. "You haven't been drinking sugar juice have you?"

"Who us?" said Yellow Belly breezily, "never."

Sheila and Moonbeam harnessed themselves while Pobo unmoored the ship and they began to pull off into the gentle lapping waves, warmed by the tropical sun. Before long Rough Town receded into a hazy smudge on the horizon. For several more days the animals had a pleasant journey. Pobo kept them entertained with his stories of strange lands he had visited on previous voyages. During the day it got pretty hot and Yellow Belly was torn between his need to cool down and his fear of swimming in the ocean. *There could be sharks, sea monsters and god knows what else.* Eventually it got too hot and he did take the dive. Sheila and Moonbeam unharnessed themselves to play in the water with him. Once Yellow Belly got over his fear, he even enjoyed himself.

"You know," said Yellow Belly afterward, "I think I could hear the dolphins. It was like they were talking in beeps and clicks."

On the dawn of the fifth day they saw a new land rising over the horizon. It appeared at first as a shining mountain rising up out of the sea.

"That'll be Parrot Island," said Pobo.

As they drew closer they could see a dark green jungle surrounding the mountain and flocks of birds rising from it, screeching.

Chapter 7 -
A Warm Welcome

As the ship drew closer to the land and the deep jungle rose up to meet them, the animals fell silent wondering what was awaiting them. Sheila and Moonbeam pulled the ship toward a muddy strip of shore. A flock of parrots flew to meet them. They were red and green with long beautiful tail feathers that skimmed the water.

"Welcome, Welcome," said the parrots, "Little Fox and Yellow Belly, great heroes." Yellow Belly looked pleased that they had remembered him. "Pobo, the great voyager, welcome, welcome. The High Priestess is preparing a great feast. Welcome, Welcome."

Pobo tied his ship to a sunken jungle tree and swung the gangplank down. Sheila and Moonbeam poked their heads out of the water and waved goodbye with their flippers as the three animals walked off the gangplank, accompanied by the swooping parrots. More parrots joined them as they entered the steamy mossy jungle, filled with beautiful flowers, huge ferns, and the striped pillars of palm trees.

"Some place, huh," whispered Yellow Belly to Little Fox.

"It's amazing," said Little Fox "though I do find it rather warm. I guess I'm more of a cold loving animal."

"Oh its deliciously warm," said Yellow Belly.

At length they came to big clearing in the jungle, surrounded by huge trees. The clearing was filled with all kinds of parrots. There were big red and green ones. There were duller green parrots with bright yellow crests. There were long tailed lorikeets, blue macaws, tiny yellow budgies, and big white cockatoos. There were big fat flightless parrots, and in the middle, standing on a golden perch was a sleek black parrot, with gold necklaces and gold rings.

"Welcome," said the sleek black parrot. "I am Nala, high priestess of all parrots. In the name of Kaka the Screecher, I welcome you, mammal, reptile and monotreme. There is much to talk about. But you must be hungry after your long journey so first let us eat. We have food for herbivores, carnivores and insectivores."

There was a flutter among the parrots and they drew off into the shadows of the trees returning with baskets of different food in their beaks. There were baskets of grubs and insects, nuts and a dizzying array of different fruits the likes of which Yellow Belly and Little Fox had never seen. There was stuff

for the carnivores: roasted mice, fish, and oily sliced eel. There were gourds with different fruit juices, waters and teas, there were even some gourds filled with sugar juice that Yellow Belly eyed greedily.

To Little Fox it all smelled delicious.

Chapter 8 -
The High Priestess

The parrots sat perched contentedly around the clearing as night fell, one parrot flew around lighting the fires, and a flock of silvery blue macaws performed a dance in the firelight. When the performance had finished the High Priestess fluttered over to Little Fox. She looked very striking, all iridescent black, covered in gold decorations, necklaces and rings.

"I trust our hospitality has been to your liking."

Little Fox yawned and licked his lips. "The best."

The High Priestess cocked her head. "How soon do you think you could start your mission?"

"I suppose I should start tomorrow."

"Oh you are a great hero indeed," said the High Priestess. "I hardly believed it possible when I heard you were arriving on our shores. Do you have a plan?"

Little Fox shook his head. "I feel awfully out of my depth to be honest. I'm of course flattered that all you parrots hold me in such high regard and expect so much of me. But really I'm just quite an ordinary little fox. I think it's absolutely terrible that your island is sinking into the sea, and I'll help in anyway that I can. But I have no magic and I don't know how I'm going to do anything to stop your island from sinking. Have you got any idea where to start?"

The High Priestess nodded seriously. "You are brave. I do have an idea of a place to start. The Sacred Mountain has awakened. Some days smoke billows from its summit. Explosions and booms can be heard from its depths. The Feathered God is angry. The parrots are too afraid to enter the cave that leads to the mountain's molten

heart where the Feathered God dwells. But you are not a parrot. You can enter the cave without fear. For you it is not forbidden. Perhaps in the cave you will find out what is making the gods angry."

"I see," said Little Fox, "I guess that seems like a good place to start. How do we get to there?"

"It is no problem," replied the parrot in a soft voice. She cast her eyes around the figures illuminated by the firelight and locked eyes on a fat round parrot who was still stuffing herself on a basket of grubs. The priestess lifted her wing and beckoned her to join them. The fat round parrot pulled herself to her feet and wandered over.

"May, I introduce," said the priestess, "Green Bum, keeper of the lore."

The fat parrot bowed.

"At your service." Little Fox returned the bow

"Green Bum," continued the priestess "is a kakapo, she can't fly but she likes to eat. Her folk live close to the sacred cave and usually don't

36

come down to us lowland dwellers. She will be your guide."

Green Bum looked nervously around and stuffed another grub into her mouth.

"Fantastic," said Little Fox. "It's all sorted then. We'll leave first thing tomorrow."

Chapter 9 -
A Walk through the Jungle

Little Fox, Yellow Belly and Green Bum set off
the next morning. At first they waded through the

swampy sunken forest. Bright coloured spiders crawled out of the way and large iridescent butterflies fluttered in the gloom of the forest floor. Green Bum appeared to be rather gloomy herself, pausing only to snap and swallow down insects as they walked. They paused for a break, resting among the buttressed roots of a big rainforest tree. In the afternoon they made it out of the sunken forest. The jungle became lighter, dominated by palms, ferns and moss. Big golden beetles and small blue bees buzzed between large succulent flowers. On they trudged, Green Bum following narrow muddy trails that brought them inevitably upward.

"Not much of a talker, our guide, is she?" said Yellow Belly.

"I heard that," said Green Bum gloomily. "I do my job, but I don't have to pretend to like it."

Yellow Belly rolled his eyes. "Why are you so sad? Aren't you happy like the rest of them that we heroes are here to save you?"

"You seem like nice animals," said Green Bum. "Soon we'll break out of these bushes and you'll have a nice view of the bay."

"Was she trying to change the subject?" Yellow Belly whispered in Little Fox's ear.

"Just leave her alone," said Little Fox. "She's obviously upset about something and you calling her a fat flightless blob is not helping."

"If you say so," said Yellow Belly, "but I'm going to get the bottom of it."

"Stop your whispering and gossiping," said Green Bum. "We have still got a long way to go before we camp for the night."

Soon, as Green Bum had promised, they broke out of the thick jungle and onto a rocky out crop. The light rain had lifted and they had an amazing view over the steaming jungle and to the lapping ocean beyond.

"Storm's coming," said Green Bum dully.

"How do you know?" asked Little Fox. "It looks like a nice day to me."

"Too nice," replied the parrot. "See those big waves with white crests rolling in. They're coming from some storm out at sea, and I'd bet my tail feathers it's headed our way."

"Are you sad that you can't fly," asked Yellow

Belly.

"Feathered goddess no," said Green Bum. "Who would want to fly? It's a waste of energy. Now please stop talking and leave a parrot to her thoughts."

Into the evening they trekked higher up the mountain. The jungle became more stunted and gave way to patches of grassland.

"I'm tired," said Little Fox. "Let's have dinner and camp here for the night."

"Very well," said Green Bum.

All of a sudden the mountain rumbled and the ground beneath them gently shook. The animals looked up at the imposing mountain. A black plume

of smoke rose billowing into the sky, momentarily blocking out the sun and casting the animals into shadow.

"The Feathered God is angry," said Green Bum sadly. "The island is sinking. We are all doomed."

Chapter 10 - Green Bum's Warning

Little Fox woke in the early morning. It was dark but the embers of their campfire still glowed. Green Bum sat on a slab of rock not far away, muttering softly to herself. Little Fox pricked up his ears. He, perhaps even more than other foxes, had extraordinarily good hearing. If he strained he could hear the beating sound of a butterfly's wings. And though no doubt Green Bum believed she was not being heard, Little Fox could hear her as clearly as if she had been sitting right beside him.

"I can't tell them…" Green Bum said. "But they are such nice animals…" she moaned. "But the Feathered God must have her request… But it's not fair; it seems wrong… Who are you to know what is right and wrong… Well I'm me… Well go on then

43

tell them if you must… But I'll get in trouble… Well don't tell them then… Oh why did it have to be me?"

Green Bum continued in this manner until she made her way back to the glowing remains of the fire and flopped down. Little Fox allowed his ears to droop and his eyes to close.

When the sun rose and they all woke, the three animals had a breakfast of the leftovers from the feast that they had carried, wrapped in leaves, in their bindles.

"Well not far now to the Sacred Cave," said Green Bum, looking miserable. "We should be there before midday."

The mountain gave another rumble, the ground shook, and more smoke billowed into the sky. They pushed on, up the volcano along gravely paths of sharp black rock.

"Up there." Green Bum pointed a clawed toe toward a dark crack in the mountain. Up there is the Sacred Cave. You should umm…" Green Bum wouldn't meet their eyes. "You should um just go into the cave… I'm sure you will be able to find out more about what's been going on."

"Green Bum," said Little Fox, "You are really a great parrot, the best parrot we've ever known. We are really grateful for your help, but before we go in there, is there something that you would like to tell us?"

Green Bum broke down. She began to cry and wipe her eyes. "You are good animals too. I have to tell you, I have to. You've been brought here on false pretences. Do you really think Pobo couldn't find a hero closer to home? No it was trick to lure you here. The Feathered God is going to cut out your heart and eat you. You're here to save us, yes. But not as a hero, as a sacrifice."

Little Fox felt stunned. He had really liked and trusted Pobo. "Why ... why me?"

"The Feathered God asked for you. Little Fox of the Sunny Meadow. Only your blood will sate her apatite. Pobo only collected you because he loves gold and the High Priestess has already rewarded him. You really are going to your death and its all my fault." Green Bum broke down into tears.

Chapter 11 -
The Sacred Cave

Little Fox, Yellow Belly and Green Bum enjoyed the sun beside the scrubby bushes in front of the Sacred Cave.

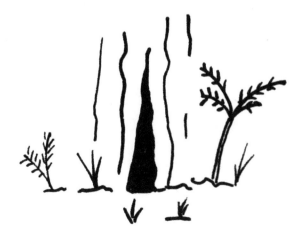

"This time I'm really not going with you," said Yellow Belly. "We've been through thick and thin but I'm not walking into a sacrifice. I'll wait here with old grub-eating Green Bum for three days and after that well… I don't know. Are you sure you want to do this?"

"I've got to find out what is going on," said Little Fox. "It doesn't make sense. Why would this 'Feathered One' ask for me? How does it know anything about me? I have to find out and if I die then I die."

Yellow Belly lifted his tail and wiped a tear out of his eye. "You really are brave."

Green Bum began to cry, wailing and blubbering. "You really are a hero, stupid but great."

"Well," said Little Fox, "wish me luck." And he stepped into the darkness.

The high crack of the cave tapered into a comfortably wide tunnel. The ground was dry and smooth. It was quiet and pitch black. Little Fox glanced behind him. The tunnel entrance was now only a slit of light. He felt a shiver of fear, but he reminded himself why he had come. Somebody had asked for him and he would find out who, so he kept padding along the tunnel.

At length he saw a light in front of him, not the pale light of day but an orange glow like fire. The passage gradually became warmer and lighter. He was able to see some of the cave around him and saw that it was covered in paintings: prints of parrot claws, paintings of parrots in different forms and feathers. The passage widened into a cavern. At the end of the cavern was a cliff that opened onto what little fox realised was the crater of the volcano. Day light streamed in from above and from below came the orange glow of lava.

"Who dares disturb the Sacred Cave," a loud voice boomed.

Little fox turned to see a large figure blocking the way he had come. It looked like a gigantic bird and was covered in feathers. His fur stood on end and he yelped in fear. But there was something, something familiar in the sound of that voice. And as he sniffed the air he detected something odd about this creature's smell. It smelled of feathers, but old feathers. And beneath that it smelled like something else, like metal.

"I am Little Fox of Sunny Meadow."

Laughter echoed in the chamber and a net fell from the ceiling, tangling Little Fox and pinning him to the floor. "Oh Little Fox, you really are the stupidest of animals. Whoever said that foxes are cunning?"

Little Fox realised where he had heard that voice before. It was the voice of Monkey, Monkey of Silver Mountain.

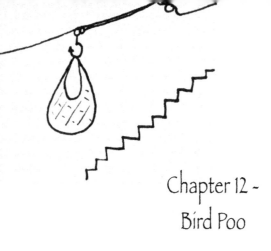

Chapter 12 -
Bird Poo

The iron claw of the feathered machine scooped up the net in which Little Fox was caught. After which a small golden shape scuttled down the machine to land on the floor in the glowing light of the lava.

"You stupid, stupid animal," said Monkey. "You really thought that the parrots of Parrot Island needed a hero?" Monkey's tone was dripping with sarcasm. "A hero," he mocked, "a hero. Not only are you stupid you are also arrogant. But now you are on an island in the middle of nowhere with no friends and you will never get out of here alive."

"But," Little Fox thought desperately as he struggled biting at the net, "but the island really is sinking, I mean I saw the sinking forest. If it's you who's causing it to sink, don't you think the parrots will find out the truth."

"Ha ha, come, Little Fox. Let me show you something."

Monkey led the way, to a corner of the chamber where a stairway, cut into the rock, led upward. The feathered machine followed with jerking mechanical movements that reminded Little Fox of the metal monkeys he had seen at the Silver Mountain. The machine transferred the net with Little Fox to a hook on a chain. He heard the clanking sound of cogs moving and the hook began to move along a track, carrying him up the stairs.

"The High Priestess of the parrots," said Monkey as he ran behind Little Fox, "knows all about my operation. She has a very sensible love of gold. But gold is not half as valuable these days as bird poo! I give her the gold; She gives me the poo. It's perfect."

The chain and hook rattled to a halt as Little Fox was pulled out of the dark tunnel into a large open area of the crater, close to the top of the mountain. On three sides it was closed by the mountain but

one side opened to the crater from which a cliff descended into a bubbling lake of lava. The rock was white and smelly. A few bedraggled looking rats and some parrots hacked at the rock face filling baskets. They attached the baskets to chains and pulleys that moved them down the steep slope on the south side of the mountain.

"Bird poo." Monkey danced with delight. "The birds have been pooing on this mountain top for hundreds of years before it became forbidden. Everybody in the world needs bird poo. It makes plants grow and makes things explode." He picked up a chunk of the white rock and threw it into the volcano. A rumbling boom and an eruption of black smoke followed. I employ traders like that silly platypus to move the rock to Rough Town where I store it in my new palace. If her island sinks a little from the explosions, it's a small price to pay for a hoard of gold and if she needs to sacrifice a few of her people to work then it is of small consequence."

"You're an evil animal," said Little Fox, still struggling in the net.

"And the best thing of all," said Monkey, shaking and shrieking with excitement, "Is that I have you, and I will have my revenge."

Chapter 13 - The Storm

Little Fox continued to struggle in the net, hanging from the hook that dangled from the chain that was fixed to the cliff.

"Stop gawking you feathered fluff balls." Monkey said menacingly to a pair of chained parrots working the cliff, "get back to work."

A cloud of powdered bird poo, floated through the net and up Little Fox's nose. The dust burned his nostrils and he began to sneeze.

"Ha ha," said Monkey. "You like that, do you?

You cross-eyed bottom-feeder, you long-nosed dumb-dumb."

Monkey picked up more of the white dust and threw it into Little Fox's face burning his eyes, nose and mouth so much that he yelped in pain.

"That is what you get," said Monkey. "That's what you get when you mess with Monkey. I'm going to shave off your fur and extract your teeth one by one. Oh the joy of vengeance!"

"You're a monster," snarled Little Fox, "and one day you'll get what's coming to you."

"Will I?" said monkey in a soft voice. "Perhaps one day we'll all get what is coming to us. But today it will be you."

"Boss, boss," one of the parrots was saying, "boss, there's a storm coming."

A dark cloud crossed the sun, throwing the vulcano into shadow. A cool wind blew away the warm air, bringing with it the smell of salt and rain. It blew the bird poo dust into little eddies. Thunder rumbled in the distance. And specks of rain began to fall from the sky."

"Curses," said Monkey, "we will have to retire

to the caves. Leave the fox out here to dangle in the rain."

Rain pounded down so that the world around Little Fox seemed to fill with water. Streams flooded through the mountain and gushed into the volcano from which steam rose hissing into the air. The wind blew the net and it swung to and fro. A powerful and sudden blast of wind roared in. It ripped the chain off its fixing against the cliff and Little Fox, still tangled in the net, fell into the rising water. He struggled to keep his nose above the surface as the dirty torrent flowed over him, pulling him toward the crater and the lava. He bit at the parts of the net that he had already weakened. But his strength was leaving him and he flailed desperately as the water washed him slowly toward the edge. Then he managed to bite a hole in the net. Lightening smashed from the sky. And thunder rumbled over the Island. Little Fox scrambled out of the net and up on to a rock to avoid the flow of water.

He cast his eye around, looking for an escape route. If he ran back into the tunnels Monkey would catch him. *There must be another way to escape*, he thought. Just then he spotted a path, it was difficult, but possible, to climb up the cliff and over the edge of the crater to freedom. Struggling, through the rain and wind, nearly being blown to his doom, Little Fox somehow made it to the summit of the mountain and looked out at the island as the storm broke over it.

Chapter 14 -
Green Bum's Hut

Looking back, Little Fox could see the bird poo mine filling with water while the volcano hissed, steamed and rumbled. He took a deep breath in and began to climb down the mountain jumping from rock to

rock but everything was getting caught up in an avalanche of gravel and water and he found himself hurtling down the volcano. *Oh no*, he thought, *I'm going to crash*. The mudslide carried him straight into the trunk of an old jungle tree. He hit his head and fell unconscious.

When he awoke, he found himself beside a warm fire, curled up on a dry wooden floor. He looked groggily around. He was in a wooden hut with a roof of huge leaves. Raindrops spattered off the roof. It felt comfortable inside.

"Look," said a familiar voice. "He's awake." It was Yellow Belly.

"Well, thank the Feathered One for that." It was the voice of Green Bum. "Here you go, you old mammal, drink up this bowl of hot coconut milk. Little fox smelled the strange smell of coconut milk. It was like nothing he had smelled before. He whisked out his tongue and tasted it. It tasted so good. He suddenly realised how hungry he was, and lapped the whole bowl up. Before long he was starting to feel himself again.

"How long have I been here for?" he asked.

"The kakapos found you yesterday morning," said Yellow Belly. "We brought you back here and Green Bum and I have been looking after you. There was a big storm, a lot of trees have come down, and there is flooding all over the place. The parrots have been in a state, fixing their houses. Also the island sank again."

"It's worse then that," said Green Bum in a low a voice. "The High Priestess has said that the gods are angry, that you offended them, and that you need to be caught and killed. The parrot war party is on their way. The war queen, Blue Feather, is commanding. They are planning to cut you into pieces to placate the gods."

"It's not true." Little Fox got up and began to pace around the room. "You know who is really behind all this? Monkey. Monkey is inside the volcano mining bird poo. He's paid off the high priestess with gold. And enslaved some of the parrots. Pobo lied to us. This whole thing was a trap to get us here because Monkey wants revenge."

"Oh noooo," said Yellow Belly with a wail, "we'll never get off this island."

Chapter 15 -
The War Party

Green Bum's hut was built on stilts and had a wooden balcony looking out over the palms and ferns. Green Bum, Yellow Belly and Little Fox stood on the balcony and watched the war party emerge from the jungle. The strongest parrots were prepared for battle carrying in their talons spears and wearing bronze helmets. They flew from tree to tree, weighed down with their armour and weapons. The High Priestess flew among them, wearing a golden helmet. She flew into the palm tree in the front of the hut.

"There they are," she squawked, "and there is the traitor, Green Bum. Get them. Get them."

Yellow Belly hissed and showed his fangs. "Come

at me, you pigeons."

There was a flutter of wings and the war party flew at the hut. Green Bum lifted her neck back and let out a cry, a strange kind of booming noise. "Stop," said Green Bum in a deep booming voice so unlike what Little Fox and Yellow Belly were used to. "Let's not shed blood. Little Fox came from across the world to aid us. Should we not listen to his story?"

The High Priestess lifted off from the branch and flew into the air. Her voice was clear and loud.

"Green Bum has betrayed us. We shall not listen to foreigners and traitors. Take them. Kill them. Beat them. Skewer them. Have no mercy."

At that moment the volcano rumbled and smoke belched into the sky.

"Doom, doom," screeched the High Priestess. "The gods are angry the island is sinking. Tarry not. Come, destroy them before the gods destroy us."

"Wait." said a big bright blue parrot, the war queen Blue Feather. "We never attack without first performing our war dance. It would be an insult to the gods. "Come warriors dance."

The warrior parrots flew, shrieking, up into the air. They wheeled, summersaulted and threw up their spears and caught them. "Death," they sang, "death to our enemies."

"I'm not your enemy," shouted Little Fox. "But Monkey is."

The blue parrot paused while keeping herself aloft. "Monkey?" she sang, "but I thought we had driven away that devil years ago."

"Well he's back," said Little Fox. "He's pretending to be the Feathered One but its really just one of his magical machines. He's enslaved some parrots, and is mining the ancient sacred bird poo. That is what is causing the mountain to sink and causing the explosions!"

"I could just about believe that of that devious beast."

"Lies," cried out the High Priestess, "lies, lies, the mammal lies."

"Monkey has been paying the High Priestess off with his gold. I bet she hasn't told you where she's been getting all her gold. Come to the Sacred Cave and see for yourself."

"Hmm," said Blue Feather, "but the rules state that only the High Priestess has the power to enter the Sacred Cave."

Green Bum cleared her throat. "Well, technically, as the keeper of the lore, I can say that in a time of turmoil the war queen is permitted to enter the Sacred Cave with a retinue of followers and I would say that the current circumstances qualify as turmoil."

"Very well then," said Blue Feather. "We shall see the truth for ourselves."

The warrior parrots repeated the sentiment in unison. "See the truth, see the truth."

"Fools," cried the High Priestess, "idiots the gods will be angry at you and consume you all." The black parrot circled around the hut before flying off into the jungle.

Chapter 16 -
The Chase

Little Fox, Yellow Belly, Green Bum, Blue Feather and the warrior parrots approached the cave. From within they could hear the rumbling of the volcano.

"You sure about the rules?" Blue Feather asked Green Bum.

The flightless Parrot nodded. "It is my job to know."

The war queen looked a little afraid. "Well here goes."

She stepped into the cave and little Fox went after, feeling a shiver of fear himself as he reentered the cave. The other animals trooped silently into the darkness. At length they all came to the glowing cavern where the feathered machine stood.

"Who dares disturb the Scared Cave of the

Feathered God?" rang out a booming voice.

The parrots drew back in fear.

"You're not a god," shouted Little Fox, "You're a machine." He ran at the machine and jumped at it, biting onto cloth and feathers. He pulled at the cloth while the machine flailed. He fell to the ground, pulling the feathered cloak with him, revealing the machine with Monkey sitting at its head.

"Our sacred cloak," screamed the parrots. "Defiler, defiler, get him."

Monkey looked wide-eyed at the parrot warriors flew at him throwing their spears and shrieking in anger. Monkey ran up the stairs, the parrots, Little Fox and Yellow Belly close behind. Past the entrance to the lava chamber they ran and up into the open bird-poo-mine.

"Defiler, defiler" screeched the parrots, "get him."

Monkey ran on, following the path that little Fox had used up the cliff to the volcano's summit. But the parrots were faster. Flying up the slope, they surrounded him. Monkey grabbed a bag of exploding white rock from his belt, and lit it with a magic snip of his fingers. An explosion rocked the side of the mountain and warrior parrots fell back.

"Ha," shouted monkey "You are no match for me."

He raced down the mountain slope, as the animals regrouped behind him and continued the pursuit. When he reached the forest, he swung from tree to tree or scuttled on all fours along the branches. The parrots flew after him, shrieking their war cries, while Little Fox ran along the ground, Yellow Belly on his back.

Again the parrots nearly had him but he pulled more white rock from his belt. Explosions rocked the jungle, felling trees. At length Monkey made it to the high black cliffs on the south side of the Island beneath which waves crashed against the rocks. The parrots, Little Fox and Yellow Belly raced to the edge, cornering Monkey against the cliff. All his white rock was gone.

"Give up," said Little Fox. "We have you now. You can't run any further"

The parrots lowered their spears and began to close in.

There was a wild, mad look in Monkey's eyes.
"We are not done yet you stupid canine."
Monkey jumped.

Chapter 17 - Dolphin Whispering

Little Fox, Yellow Belly and the parrots gathered around the edge of the cliff. Monkey fell, his body straight like a tree. The white-topped waves smashed against the cliff and there, rocking in the bay, was a familiar ramshackle boat, loaded high with baskets of white rock. Pobo the platypus was playing with his ropes, a black parrot dressed in gold perched on the mast, and the two dolphins, Sheila and Moonbeam, frolicked in the water. Little Fox watched as Monkey crashed into the foaming water, and resurfaced gasping for breath. Pobo threw him a rope and monkey scrambled aboard the ship.

"That old pirate," said Yellow Belly. "I knew he was a good for nothing dung smuggler and now he's escaping with the other two villains. We'll see about

that." Yellow Belly sped toward the edge of the cliff.

"Wait," screamed Little Fox, "what are you doing? Stop!"

But Yellow Belly's answer could not be heard as he shot into the air and arced downward toward the water. Little Fox watched in horror as his freind fell then dived into the water just as the ship was pulling away from the land. Little Fox stood by the cliff for a long time waiting for Yellow Belly to reappear. But he saw nothing and with a heavy heart eventually turned his back on the ocean and the cliffs. Would he ever see his friend again?

Over the next few days the parrots began to put the island to right. Monkey's machines and mining operations were cast into the volcano. Green Bum, who, thanks to her courage, became the new high priestess, blessed the ground. She also blessed the scared cave and a new sacred cloak of feathers was made for the gods. Little Fox was made a welcome guest and feasted on delicious fish and bowls of coconut milk. The parrots also made a small cloak of colorful feathers and gave it to Little Fox as reward for uncovering the truth. After the mining work stopped the mountain seemed to calm. There were few rumblings and the island stopped sinking into the sea.

Despite all this Little Fox couldn't help but feel sad. It had been so brave of Yellow Belly to jump off the cliff like that, but where was he now? Had he drowned or been killed by Monkey, Pobo and the old high priestess. As days wore on Little Fox became more and more worried. Then another thought occurred to him. Without Pobo and his boat he had no way to get off the island and get home. He liked the parrots and he liked Parrot Island. But he missed the meadow and that was where he belonged. He began to feel sad and there was nothing the parrots could do to cheer him.

One morning, Little Fox was standing by the sea gazing toward the horizon when Yellow Belly popped his head out of the ocean and slithered on to the beach.

"Hello old friend," he said, "I'm back."

"Yellow Belly!" cried Little Fox. "Where have you been? How did you survive?"

"I've been swimming with the dolphins," said

Yellow Belly, "they are really quite talkative you know, not bad creatures. I told them all about our adventures and what had been happening on Parrot Island and they told me all about life as a dolphin. I can tell you, those two are not too happy with their old friend Pobo! They abandoned his ship to drift on the ocean currents. It will probably come apart in a storm. And now Sheila and Moonbeam have come back with me."

Little Fox looked out at the water and saw the dorsal fins of two dolphins gliding in the shallows.

"They've agreed to take us home," said Yellow Belly. "Just think of it, home. We've just got to build a boat."